D0445361

A NOTE TO PARENTS

Disney's First Readers Level 2 books were created for beginning readers who are gaining confidence in their early reading skills.

Compared to Level 1 books, **Level 2** books have slightly smaller type and contain more words to a page. Although sentence structure is still simple, the stories are slightly longer and more complex.

Just as children need training wheels when learning to ride a bicycle, they need the support of a good model when learning to read. Every time your child sees that you enjoy reading, whether alone or with him or her, you provide the encouragement needed to build reading confidence. Here are some helpful hints to use with the **Disney's First Readers Level 2** books:

★ Play or act out each character's words. Change your voice to indicate which character is speaking. As your child becomes comfortable with the printed text, he or she can take a favorite character's part and read those passages.

★ Have your child try reading the story. If your child asks about a word, do not interrupt the flow of reading to make him or her sound it out. Pronounce the word for your child. If, however, he or she begins to sound it out, be gently encouraging—your child is developing phonetic skills!

★ Read aloud. It's still important at this level to read to your child. With your child watching, move a finger smoothly along the text. Do not stop at each word. Change the tone of your voice to indicate punctuation marks, such as questions and exclamations. Your child will begin to notice how words and punctuation marks make sense and can make reading fun.

★ Let your child ask you questions about the story. This will help to develop your child's critical thinking skills. Use the After-Reading Fun activities provided at the end of each book as a fun exercise to further enhance your child's reading skills.

★ Praise all reading efforts warmly and often!

Remember that early-reading experiences that you share with your child can help him or her to become a confident and successful reader later on!

— Patricia Koppman
Past President
International Reading Association

First published by Disney Press, New York, New York.
This edition published by Scholastic Inc.,
90 Old Sherman Turnpike, Danbury, Connecticut 06816
by arrangement with Disney Licensed Publishing.

SCHOLASTIC and associated logos are trademarks of Scholastic Inc.

ISBN 0-7172-6467-X

Printed in the U.S.A.

Hide-and-Seek

by Kathryn Cristaldi
Illustrated by Sol Studios

Disney's First Readers — Level 2
A Story from Disney's *Pocahontas*

SCHOLASTIC INC.

New York Toronto London Auckland Sydney
Mexico City New Delhi Hong Kong Buenos Aires

Pocahontas loved the forest.
She played there every day.
Her favorite game was hide-and-seek.
Before she'd hide she'd say—

"I'm as swift as a river.
I'm as strong as a tree.
I'm as fast as the wind blows.
You will never find me!"

Pocahontas had a good friend,
and John Smith was his name.
One day the friends agreed to play
their very own hide-and-seek game.

John Smith smiled from ear to ear.
He knew that he would win.
"You may go first," he told his friend.
"Get ready! Let's begin!"

"I'm as swift as a river.
I'm as strong as a tree.
I'm as fast as the wind blows.
You will never find me!"

Was she hiding by the oak tree?
Was she curled up in a log?
John Smith heard a deep voice singing.
CROAK! It was just a frog!

Was she hiding by the bushes?
Now there was something funny.
John Smith saw two eyes blinking.
No, it was just a bunny!

He climbed up a mountain.
Something moved over there.
John Smith looked in a
dark, old cave.
Oh, no! A big brown bear!

"I'm as swift as a river.
I'm as strong as a tree.
I'm as fast as the wind blows.
You never found me!"

"The hiding part is easy,"
John Smith called to his friend.
"Now I will hide, and you will find
that I'll win in the end."

John Smith dove under a waterfall.
He would be well hidden there.
But John Smith was not like a fish,
He needed to get air!

Buried under a pile of leaves,
he found the perfect spot.
John Smith felt a tickle.
ACHOO! Well, maybe not!

He hung from a leafy tree branch.
That's one place he had not tried.
Then . . . *CRACK!*
The tree branch snapped in two.
There was no place left to hide!

When Pocahontas stopped laughing,
John Smith agreed she'd won.
Hide-and-seek was not that easy . . .

But it sure was
lots of fun!

AFTER-READING FUN

Enhance the reading experience with follow-up questions to help your child develop reading comprehension and increase his/her awareness of words.

Approach this with a sense of play. Make a game of having your child answer the questions. You do not need to ask all the questions at one time. Let these questions be fun discussions rather than a test. If your child doesn't have instant recall, encourage him/her to look back into the book to "research" the answers. You'll be modeling what good readers do and, at the same time, forging a sharing bond with your child.

Hide-and-Seek

1. **What was Pocahontas' favorite game?**

2. **With whom did Pocahontas play hide-and-seek?**

3. **Why do you think Pocahontas knew the best place to hide?**

4. **What is your favorite game? How do you play it?**

5. **What living things were in the forest?**

6. **How many pairs of rhyming words can you find in the story?**

Answers: 1. hide-and-seek. 2. her good friend, John Smith. 3. she knew the forest very well because she played there every day. 4. answers will vary. 5. possible answers: trees, mushrooms, frog, bear, raccoon, birds, rabbits, butterflies, plants, ants. 6. possible answers: day-say; tree-me; name-game; win-begin; log-frog; funny-bunny; there-bear; there-air; friend-end; spot-not; tried-hide; won-fun.